FORGEMASTERS OF THE REALM

CORONATION

SNÆBJÖRN

ISBN: 978-1-4669-8648-0 (sc)
ISBN: 978-1-4669-8650-3 (hc)
ISBN: 978-1-4669-8649-7 (e)

Library of Congress Control Number: 2013906072

Trafford rev. 04/01/2013

 www.trafford.com

North America & international
toll-free: 1 888 232 4444 (USA & Canada)
phone: 250 383 6864 ♦ fax: 812 355 4082

CONTENTS

PRELUDE

The world was in total chaos, with the shattering of ancient allegiances, and war had started. Many villages had been destroyed, leaving behind nothing but columns of refugees, which clogged the roadways. Cries filled the countryside, seeking lost family members or the loss of lives of inhabitants. The countryside thoroughfares were reduced to puddles of mud because of the exiles trying to vie with the columns of soldiers as they were trying to reach the frontlines. The capitals of Hearthglen and Vokva had swollen beyond the breaking point as the sheer number of refugees had caused shortages of housing, medicines, and food. Not since the Great Rendering War had the peoples of the world experienced such a breakdown in society.

But there was hope—eternal hope—for hope is the great invisible force in the universe. Agnar and his band of merrymen had reforged the sword Mjolnir. If the sword can make it into the hands of the dark elves, the allegiance could be reactivated. Between the race of men, the dwarves, and the elven race, there was hope.

Helgi the Gray and Baldur had reached the Kingdom of Jotheim, having had raced against time, speeding at a full pace. They requested an audience with King Smakongur after many insistences and finally had been accepted into the audience chamber. Before them sat King Smakongur at a table lined up with various fruits and drinks. The guests went through the proper greetings out of courtesy for the king. Baldur stared at the king, examined his portly stature, and noticed his regal attire. '*Odd that he seems so oblivious to the events in his realm,*' thought Baldur. Baldur and Helgi the Gray were standing in the middle of the room, when the king said coldly, "I know why you are here. I expect that you must be tired from your trek. Sit and dine with me while we talk. But you must know that I am not inclined toward your trip. I know who you are"—he was pointing toward Helgi—"but this Baldur, I know not."

Helgi the Gray and Baldur bowed and accepted a seat at the table and began to sample the food before them. Baldur introduced himself as the commander of the guards for the realm of men. "Sire, about Ft.

Windswept, I . . ." spoke Baldur, which was silenced with a wave of the hand by King Smakongur.

"What about the fort? Must we accept your meddling with the local populace in the area? We have heard of their terrorizing the local gnomes," stated the king as he stared down toward the plate before him. Baldur was staring in disbelief at the king with juices and spittle running down the king's chin.

Helgi the Gray interrupted the king with "Dost thou not know of the coming war? At this moment, gnomes in your kingdom are at a greater danger than from our soldiers."

The king stared toward Helgi the Gray, and with a pointing finger, he stated firmly, "Aye, I know of you and your actions—a troublemaker at best! Of what business do you have concerning this kingdom? For too long has the race of men instigated problems. Your foolish war was started by you. It has nothing to do with gnomes. You are welcome as guests. Rest up, and be gone with you. We will not participate in your foolish endeavors."

Baldur replied, "But what is to come of the fort? We have dispatched reinforcements . . . will you hinder their travels?"

King Smakongur pondered for a moment then said, "Nay, I will not hinder their travels as long as they stray not from the roadways to the fort. Should they deviate from the lanes, I will have my men arrest them, and then the fort will be disbanded. Do I make it clear to you?"

Helgi silently shook his head toward Baldur as if to say "Don't argue with the king, we have received his intentions."

"Surely you understand that your kingdom is in peril, but I will accept your position, and we will abide as you wish," replied Baldur sourly.

"Excellent . . . Is there anything else that you need until you depart?" asked king Smakongur.

Helgi bowed toward the king and asked, "I beseech you for assistance, perchance if I can borrow a flugapet. Baldur needs to get to Castle Vokva in the dwarven realm . . . I can pay for the ride, of course."

"Yes, yes, if only to be rid of you," King Smakongur replied bluntly. "I expect you to be leaving before sunset. And you, Helgi, will you be leaving as well?"

"Aye, sire, I am going to Woodbranch as I have a meeting to attend," replied Helgi the Gray.

Stephan and his men had reached Bátslipa just as the sun was slipping into its nightly sleep. A light dusting of snow was upon the ground, but no winds or bad weather. The village was eerily silent as most of the inhabitants dared not brave the night because of the recent horde activities. Docked at the pier were one schooner and several ferries, with a few villagers attending to the boats. Stephan had dismounted his troops to let them stretch their legs and eat before embarking to the other shore. Stephan engaged the workers around the boats, hoping to hear some news of the recent incursions by the north. Commander Stephan finally located a captain to pilot the schooner and workers for the ferries. The soldiers would use the schooner, and the mules laden with supplies will be crossed via the ferries.

Stephan returned to his men and ordered them to camp for the night. "We leave before sunrise. Expect a whole day will be consumed in loading and unloading our men and supplies. Lost precious time, but we have no choice."

The troops spent the evening mingling with the local militia. There was occasional laughter and lots of stories about military exploits. The troops found out that very seldom had soldiers from Fort Laekur been seen here. Occasionally, supplies and the odd replacements from the realm of men came by, but it was not very often. When the subject was the fort to the north, Windswept, the villagers would roll their eyes and say words like "I'm glad I'm not going with you" with a shudder. They all had heard rumors about the dark forces to the north. But here, they were subjected to bandits and orc-raiding parties, but nothing like the area around Fort Windswept. Occasionally, they could see a few puffs of smoke off in the distance, probably the result of a village that had been attacked.

Just before sunrise, Stephan gathered his troops for the march down to the schooner. He was inspecting the troops as they walked onto the gangplank, occasionally adjusting their armor with a friendly slap on the back. It took almost two hours before all of the soldiers were aboard and then he supervised the supplies ferries. Once all was ready to sail, Stephan joined the captain aboard the schooner. Shouts of "cast off" were heard as the workers labored with the guy lines. It took three hours to reach the other shore, and another three more hours to disembark the mules and supplies.

Stephan paid for the ferry service and told his men to "mount up." He rode down the line of mounted troops, inspecting each one again. The occasional soldier had a fearful look upon his face to which Stephan tried to console him. It was now that they were ashore; the reality had started to creep upon them, and it was as if they were washed in fear. The seasoned veterans could hide the fact that they were about to face combat, while the younger new recruits displayed a look of uncertainty. "Soldier up," Stephan spoke in gruff and loud voice.

"Forward, *march*!" he ordered.

It took them a day and a half, marching at full speed, to reach Windswept. Occasionally, they rode past some burned villages, some bodies in the fields, some dead cattle, and a few belongings from the inhabitants. As they neared the fort, the troop trumpeter blew a few blasts just to let the fort know that they were coming. The fortress's walls were lined with soldiers with shouts of elation with the coming reinforcements.

With the reinforcements inside of the fort and the gates secured, Stephan ordered the troops to dismount. He walked up to the fort commander, saluted, and then said, "Command Stephan, reporting as ordered!"

Rikard was greeted by the fort commander named Arnar in a rude manner. Arnar had been drinking, and his attire was disheveled and unprofessional. When Rikard advised that he was the new fort commander, Arnar fell into profanity and seemed to be glad of riddance of the position. Apparently, Arnar was not pleased and became belligerent and declined to assist Rikard. To that, Rikard said, "Fine, but I warn you here and now, if you cower under fire or you disobey my orders, I'll have you in irons. Do I make it perfectly clear to you? Now, line up the troops for an inspection, and that means you along with them! Oh, one other thing, you will be housed in the barracks along with the troops, so remove your things after the inspection."

Rikard was a no-nonsense commander. He totally and clearly stated to the troops assembled before him that the fort will be run as a military station. He instructed the fort smithy to gather the weapons and armors and to make them suitable for combat. He then ordered all soldiers of the fort to stay out of the local village except when on official business. The troops were to remain attired as a soldier and to conduct themselves *as soldiers*. Some grumbles were heard within the ranks, but most of them were glad that changes have been made. He dismissed the formation and began to make plans for the fort. Everything would be combat ready: new supplies for the soldiers, patrols about the fort would be increased, and most importantly, he intended to convince the deserters in the Gate-Pass area to return to duty. He intended to offer the same deal that Baldur gave to Rikard at Hearthglen—same amnesty, same rank and duties, same honor.

Gagns and Foringi had returned to Fort Hermana, and they were glad to be back. "F-f-finally, my own b-bed to sleep in," stammered Gagns. It was good to see Boar's Head Inn again and see to old friends and hear their voices.

"Aye, 'tis good to be back home," replied Commander Foringi. "Maybe I will go to Boar's Head for dinner." He chuckled, then he added, "But first, I need to check up on the defenses of the fort and into the accommodations for our 'guests'—all the refugees. Shall we say we meet there in about five hours?"

Gagns agreed and parted ways with Commander Foringi. On the way to the inn, he started to think toward Agnar and others. *Are they alive? Is the sword reforged? How can they escape since Snjofell perished and the bridge was destroyed?* A myriad of questions popped into his head.

Commander Foringi was atop the fortress walls, surveying the area toward Blafjall Mountains and Sko Forest. He was wondering *if* the bonfires will ever be lit, signaling Agnar that his task had been successful. He had inspected the defenses and found them to be adequate. Now, he climbed down from the defensive walls and headed toward the revetment camp for the refugees. He was worried if they had enough supplies to withstand a long siege.

After the inspections were finished, between the talks with refugees and soldiers, the appointment with Gagns was almost upon him. A scrutiny of the evening skies left him at ease as the weather had improved over the last few days, and it would be spring within a week or so. *Good news to hear of* something *was finally coming our way.*

Gagns and Foringi were enjoying a leg of lamb washed down with plenty of mead. They were engaged in small talk, fort defenses, refugees, and supplies. Both of them were worried about their companions in the old citadel and the forge. Commander Foringi changed the subject to deflect their worries and asked, "Have you checked on the Konglos? Biggy will never forgive us if anything happens to them." *Ouch, that was a stupid thing to say*, he thought as he bit his tongue.

Biggy offered up his plan to everyone in the dwelling. "Simple, really. Let me order the queen Konglo to have her workers repair the bridge. Then we can get out the same way that we came in. *Plus* we can transport everyone here—the darlings and everyone—on their backs. They can walk on the web, but no one else can, including the Orcs, Ogres, and Goblins! We just walk across the crevasse over the web bridge, no?"

Dabs stood with his jaw agape, and Agnar suddenly grabbed Biggy by his shoulders, and he planted a kiss on the forehead of Biggy. "Brilliant, just brilliant!" yelled Dabs. SiSi added, "Aye, I knew ye were good for something," and Smari was pumping his hands, laughing. Only Loftur and his family and the darlings were hesitant. After all, don't the Konglos eat his darlings?

The bleating of flat trumpets was the only reason they succumbed to the idea. Dabs said to Loftur, "Gather only the essentials and prepare to leave, *and fast*." Biggy had already blinked toward the exit to reach out for assistance from the queen.

Biggy had been gone for a half an hour and returned to find everyone packing up and getting ready to leave. The queen had sent thirty-five workers toward the destroyed bridge and was on the way to the beleaguered dwellers. "Don't insult the queen. She is the only way out of here," said Biggy toward the darlings. "You need not fear them as long as you don't make them angry toward the Kongos," added Biggy.

Agnar, accompanied by Bangsi, rushed toward the howls from the north minions. Attafot joined them, along with SiSi and Dabs. Agnar said, "We must stem the assault to buy time until they can board the transports. Smari, help them load up the Konglos when they get here. We need everyone aboard and fast."

Attafot began spraying the tunnel with webbing so that the dark forces would be slowed down. Agnar, loaded with multi-arrows, filled the tunnel with a deadly spread of arrows while SiSi attempted to add another ward stone to hinder their onslaught from the Orcs. They were just buying some time so the Darlings and Loftur and his family could reach safety.

Within minutes, the Konglos appeared in droves. There must have been forty-five of the Konglos, all of them ready to service the beleaguered group. Smari loaded two darlings, burdened by their possessions, on a Konglo, and shooed them away to safety. They still needed to have seventy more seats before the last inhabitants were safely secured.

The Konglos were fast, mean really *fast*. Within ten minutes, the first bunch of evacuees had been unloaded, and the Konglos rushed backed to pick up more of them. The last of the Darlings and the Loftur family had been spirited away out of harm's way. The remaining team was retreating toward the entrances of the old citadel under constant attack from arrows. Attafot secured the exit while Agnar offered cover fire while they withdrew. Of course, Bangsi had fallen countless numbers of the dark forces as well. The retreating team had traversed three of the staircases when the unthinkable occurred. Smari had taken an arrow in the back. Smari, with a stunned face, had fallen—fallen before the evil minions—with a cry of help upon his face. Of course, no one could save him as the Orcs had already overrun his location. Bangsi, with fangs protruding, slashing foe after foe, was barely able to contain the onslaught of the evil ones. One after another, the Orcs were downed by Agnar with his deadly bow. One more staircase to go, just one more staircase as Agnar prayed for a miracle. Attafot, with arrows protruding from his body, rushed to help, spraying webbing upon the advancing foes. SiSi cast freezing spells until she was not able to continue due to a lack of manna. Dabs, locked in deadly combat with his mighty sword, was hewing Orc combatants. The Konglos then returned after dropping their precious cargo, and they returned with a vengeance as they spewed webs along with their poisons. They had saved the party, allowing them to mount a Konglo to safety.

Eventually, the Konglos had saved the day. The Darlings were transported without event; the Loftur family was reunited, and the heroes of the band had reached to safety beyond the bridge. Everyone was elated that they had reached shelter except for the fact that Smari had fallen in combat. Dabbilus wept openly over the death of his vassal. He considered him as a son. Agnar tried to console Dabbilus but to no avail. Biggy was at a loss of words as Smari was of his own. SiSi could not offer any words of consolation; she was at a loss as well. The only good thing of consequence was that the sword could be reunited once again. Once again, the good of all must prevail, and Agnar, on konglo-back, bade good-bye as he trekked toward the bonfire to signal success. He could never atone for the death of Smari, which he bore for the rest of his days.

Without Agnar, the party set out in the direction of Castle Vokva. Dabbilus was leading the team on Konglo-back, riding toward the citadel. It was a sad moment as Agnar departed for the mountains while the other party members continued their journey toward Vokva.

Baldur greeted Magnus with open arms after his golden eagle flugapet had landed. "How was your flight?" asked King Magnus. Baldur sized up the king and instantly took a liking for the king. "Too bad there are only three or four other Flugarpets left. Between the north keep shooting them down and the natural predators . . . well, you know what I mean. Excellent transport though—fast and dependable," said the king as he shook hands with Baldur. Running his hands through his hair to "comb" his mane, which was left a mess from the flight, Baldur said, "Sire, we have much to discuss on the eve of war."

King Magnus and Baldur talked openly about the alliances and how best to defend from the black forces of the north. "We have developed a new boat—Skjaldbak, we call it—which will be devastating toward the northern naval forces. We must keep it a secret. We need all of the advantages we can muster up," added the king. "I admire you for all the changes you've made after you were promoted. We heard that Commander Rikard has really shaped up Fort Gate-Pass into a real military post, a military fort as it was intended to be."

Baldur bowed and thanked the king. "And what news do you have about Agnar and his men? You know that Agnar was stationed with me in Fort Hermana—a fine military soldier."

"Alas, I have none. You haven't met Dabbilus. No, you haven't. He is a paladin serving under me. He and his valet joined forces with Agnar, and I am worried that something evil has happened to them," said the king with a worried expression on his face. "I hope that they succeed. We need as many allies as we can produce, and I doubt it very much that the gnomes will be a trustworthy ally."

"Aye, of course, I came from there yesterday, and no truer words have you spoken concerning King Smakongur. I found him most distasteful, if I may be polite." Baldur smiled as he talked toward the king. Then Baldur added, "Helgi the Gray should be arriving at Fort Hermana on the morrow. He was going to help Agnar convince the elven people that they should renew the alliance." Changing the subject, Baldur asked how well Castle Vokva could hold out for a long siege. He spoke of the possibility of an onslaught from the Lava Gates and the Blafjall Mountains.

Something was astir. The castle guards manning the main gate were blowing their horns and yelling "*To arms*, riders!"

"By the gods, has the war reached our gates?" queried the king.

Stephan was called urgently to the north wall by his second-in-command. It was just after the sunset, but the orange glow was still hanging in the air. Climbing upon the wall, his second-in-command pointed into the distance and pronounced, "It has *started*! They have begun to march upon us!" Using a looking glass, Stephan studied the masses just outside of the Skelbaka outpost. He surmised that they numbered in the thousands: the Ápastil with their horses, a massive number of ogres, and a myriad number of goblins and trolls. Of course then, there were the despicable Orcs. It seemed that there were three columns of their troops. Each column advanced, carrying torches and commanded by an orc. Stephan focused on the trolls—two trolls per catapult and battering rams, being towed with huge ropes as the trolls struggled with the boggy tundra underneath them. Because the terrain was not favorable for columns marching, the slowness of the military formations was fortunate for the defenders. It bought some precious time for preparing the defenses.

"*To arms!*" shouted Stephan to the fort. "Ready the defenses! They will be upon us before sunrise.

Ready the catapults. I want two divisions of archers, one on the walls and the rest in the fortress grounds. Bring up the grapple hooks to knock down their ladders. You there! Bring up a squad with the staves and lances and use them to reinforce the gates!" commanded Stephan in a voice of authority. "I want to knock down the ladders before they get to the fort. And keep targeting the Orcs. They are the leaders. Without command and control, the ogres will scatter. Shower the trolls with arrows. They can't tow their catapults and battering rams when their bodies are full of arrows." Stephan reached out and put a hand on the back of his second-in-command. "Keep the men's spirits up. Talk with the men with words of inspiration. I fear many men will perish before tomorrow." He left the walls and found the messenger located near the barracks. "Take a message from me. '*It has started*.' Make haste toward Fort Laekur. They can spread the word," Stephan ordered.

In the night's darkness, Stephan tried to bolster the troops by words. He could see the troops, especially the younger ones, were caught up with fear. "Not to worry. Once you are engaging the enemy, fear is your least of worries. It will disappear. I too am scared, but I have never known a soldier who wasn't scared," spoke Stephan. Everyone he saw in the fort was on edge: speaking of mates, speaking of home, speaking of their children, and telling jokes just to calm themselves.

In the distance, the sounds of the drumbeats of war echoed in the air. The constant thumping sound of footsteps came with a cadence as though the columns moved as one. Occasionally, a distance roar pierced the night, bringing fear down upon the defenders. Slowly, ever so slowly, the torches were bearing toward them. Sometimes, the columns would stop, banging their weapons against their shields; there would be silence for a few minutes, then the churning of movement again. Stephan consoled the troops by saying, "This is a typical maneuver: trying to induce fear in the enemy. Try not to listen to it." But there was no avoidance of the sounds—constant and ugly to the ears. Every now and then, there was a bleat from trumpets in the distance, then the sounds of drumbeats followed by more trumpets blaring. Everyone at the fort knew that this would be their last day on this world.

In the commander center, Stephan was discussing the onslaught with his commanders. He knew, deep down inside, that the conflict was lost. "Perhaps we can sneak away under darkness. 'Tis enough time. The hordes are following their strategies to the letter. They won't attack until sunrise. They will camp outside of our range of firepower. I'll not wait for the evil ones to slaughter every one of us. What say you? Should we try to get to Fort Laekur? They number into the thousands, and reinforcements are coming here every day," he asked his commanders. Each person in the command post knew that Stephan's words were correct, but no one dared to utter the word *retreat*. "I will stand and perish together with any one of you, but not like this. What say you? Speak your mind. I will never brand you as a coward. Speak your true thoughts," admonished Stephan.

After the meeting in the command post, Stephan spread the word that they were to leave now, in the darkness before the first light of the sun. "Quietly now, we cannot take anything except your personal weapon. Don't dally, but don't make haste either. We need the element of surprise and the darkness of night to make distance between them. Once they detect that we have left, they will hunt us down." Stephan estimated that they would have about four hours to make a good distance between the evil ones.

The troops were mounted, about four hundred in all, and they were instructed to leave in several intervals of ten soldiers each. Like Stephan predicted, the hordes from the north had set up a camp just beyond the last bog. The Ápastil could charge but not the ground troops because of the bog. Slowly but surely, the fort emptied, with Stephan being the last one. Not a person talked, plodding along until it was safe to gallop. The defenders broke into a full gallop, heading toward Bátslipa.

The messenger had just caught the ferry, and on the way to Fort Laekur, he warned as many as he could as he galloped through the village in Bátslipa. "*War, war! The Orcs are coming!*" he screamed without stopping to talk to the villagers. The villagers started to scurry home to help with family and friends. Many of them were going to make their way farther south. Some of them decided to stay and defend their properties. The captain of the ferry pass obtained a few of the villagers to remain behind as he knew that the ferries were the only lifelines to the mainland of the Kingdom of Jotheim. Soon, the ferry boats would be overloaded with gnomes escaping the onslaught from the north.

Agnar made good time riding upon the Konglo. Unlike riding a horse, the Konglo was a smooth ride, and of course, they could climb obstacles. They were fast too. He was almost there; one more ledge and the peak were in sight. The frost line on the mountains was slowly disappearing with the coming of spring although the snows still capped the peaks. The winds had picked up; the sparse vegetation plus the eroded boulders upon the mountaintops had made the journey more difficult. Although the Konglo was hesitant because of the cold and the winds, it obeyed and continued to trek onward. Agnar was constantly checking the skies, and he was slowed twice by some wraith riders[1], but Agnar had no problem avoiding detection.

As planned, the signal bonfire was there, and it jumped to life as he ignited the flare. The fires consumed the wood with glee as the signal had been set. It took about ten minutes, and suddenly, the fires were popping up atop other peaks. Mounting the Konglo, Agnar made haste to distance him from

---

[1]   Wraith Riders: ghostly specters that ride wyverns, mostly as "eyes in the sky" for the northern minions.

the peak which he was on. The wraith riders would be investigating the fires soon, and with a feeling of elation, he said to himself, "Finally, let's go meet Bogamaður." Soon, the foothills of the Blafjall Mountains emerged, and the journey quickened. Off to his left, Agnar could see the outline of the Lava Gates. He was in familiar surroundings now, which left him with a comfortable feeling. Another few hours and Fort Hermana would be within view. But Agnar's destination wasn't the fort, so he veered toward the Sko Forest. He was in his own backyard now; he knew where the carnivorous vines were, where the traps were located.

Nearing the Blafjall Mountains' foothills once again, just ahead lay the Sko Forest. He could hear the sounds of the croaking of the wraith riders and their wyverns in the distance. He could sense the presence of the northern minions; although distant, they were there. He could feel the dangers lurking in the air. He felt a chill upon his back as he thought of it.

After several hours of riding, Agnar had arrived at his destination. A dozen or two had arrived, and there in the middle of the clearing, a stunned Agnar was staring at Bogamaður, and next to him was *Snjofell*!

The Horn of Thor sounded once again in the realm of dwarves, wielded by Dabbilus. The castle guards knew that it was not an unblemished tone from the hordes from the north, but what manners of beings were assaulting their gates? These weren't dwarves, but rather *goblins*—goblins hailing them with a dwarven horn? To their amazement, the goblins were not armed and *riding* Konglos. Baldur and King Magnus were just as surprised and taken aback, trying to ascertain what was happening. As the assaulting party neared the gates, the king instantly shouted, "*Open the gates!*" with a face of glee. His bewildered look evaporated, exclaiming, "Dabbilus!" and broke into a run toward the main gates. One by one, the Konglos were escorted by the goblins through the gate. Finally, the last four Konglos had crossed the drawbridge, and before them stood Dabbilus, Biggy, and SiSi, and an unknown dwarf with his family! The castle inhabitants were standing agog, not knowing if the goblins were friend or foe.

Baldur beamed when he welcomed the adventurers. "We have much to talk about—"

The king interrupted Baldur, and the king enveloped Dabbilus with his huge arms. "Aye, much has happened since ye left." The king hugged SiSi and Biggy and turned toward the unknown dwarf. "I be King Magnus. And who ye be?"

"Loftur Hamarsson of the Flame-keepers clan from Jarnsmiða be me name," and he introduced his family to the king. "And these are me darlings," as he pointed toward the refugees from the caverns below.

The king was astonished that before him were the last survivors of Jarnsmiða!

"Welcome be ye, sorely welcome ye all," said the king, "Bring our guests to their quarters."

After several hours of resting, the castle guests were given suitable attires and summoned before the king. A long row of tables was before them, laden with drinks, meats, fruits, and desserts. They were famished, and it was not long before everyone was lost in championship like they had known all their lives. Smiles and laughter were the orders of the day with the clanging of mugs and compliments abounded. The newfound inhabitants flooded Baldur with questions about the situation which the realm faced. Dabbilus had already retold of their harrowing experience and how they had escaped with all but one loss. Biggy had been heaped praise upon praise by Dabbilus and SiSi, but the loss of Smari dampened the conversation. The king tried to console the group, but he knew that they were feeling pangs of guilt.

By then, everyone in the southern realms knew that war had been thrust upon them. Each fortress within the realms had been dispatching messenger runners on the hour for every hour of the day, spreading the word to the inhabitants. Agnar was probably the only inhabitant that didn't know of the war. Baldur was in deep thought, not only just about Agnar, but also about the fate of Stephan and his men. He already had heard that Fort Windswept had been overrun, and that the only thing between the hordes and the southern realms was Bátslipa and Fort Laekur.

The king knew that now was the time for action. He summoned Gormur and instructed him to launch the Skjaldbak. Gormur hesitated as he knew that the boats were untested, to which the king said, "Time is not on our side. If the two ferries are lost, then we will be forced to fight on multiple fronts. Get your mages to cast portals so we can transport the Skjaldbak to them down to the ferries. Make haste, lad! It is time to bring the fight to them."

Baldur adjoined the king with his pronouncements. "I shall take leave of you whilst I join the forces in Fort Laekur. Perchance you can dispatch a runner to Hearthglen to let the queen and Lady Zonda know?"

Dabbilus nodded in acceptance of the plans and added, "I shall leave at this forthwith. I can help in Fort Gate-Pass. I know where we can find some manpower to bolster the fort."

Loftur was looking toward Baldur and asked what he and his darlings could do. "Aye, Loftur, ye can help a good deal here in the castle. Darlings would be wonderful for attending to the wounded and supplies." Not to be left behind, Baldur said, "Biggy, command the Konglos here in the castle. And you, SiSi, you can help with the children and the women, should they need to be brought into the caverns for safety."

Stephan and his men were within a half day of riding toward the ferry. He had sent two scouts back to see how far they were between the hordes. They had reported back that there were about a hundred or so after them, mostly on horseback, backed with about twenty wraith riders. With that news, Stephan ordered the column to head toward the coast. He knew that the horses would not last much longer; they need to rest. He gauged that it would be about two hours before they caught up to him and his men. If he could make it to a cove on the shoreline, then he could hold the horses there, and they could backtrack on foot and set up defensive positions there. The horses would be safe there while they rest.

Within the hour, the steeds were resting within the sanctuary of the cove. Stephan and his men were waiting away from the horses, and the defensive position had been set. He directed his warriors to line up shoulder to shoulder with their shields held outward. A squad of lancers lined behind with their javelins between the first lines of soldiers. Then another crew was behind them with their shields held over their heads. Beyond that, the archers were lined up in a circle to give cover and firepower against the wraith riders; the rest of the swordsmen were to take out any stragglers and Ápastil, if they had breached the line. It wasn't long to wait as the clouds of dust and the sounds of hooves reached nearer and nearer.

"Hold the line!" yelled Stephan as the first horsemen charged toward the men. The clash was deafening, with the sounds of the clanging of shields warding off the hooves of the horsemen. The sound of the yells and screams from injured combatants and the whinnying of the horses flew out of their throats. Horses with arrows protruding from their bodies fell down onto the line. "Hold the line, men!" Stephan screamed as he ran to replace a fallen soldier. With a swipe of his sword, he felled one of the foes. Turning around, he saw a wyvern pluck a soldier off his feet. Instinctively, Stephan leapt into action with his broadsword, which immediately cut the head of the wyvern from its torso. The archers were filling the air with arrows as volley after volley fell upon the horsemen and the wraith riders, singing through the air as a swarm of angry bees. Several soldiers had been snatched up by the wyverns, flew up and cast aside the helpless soldiers. The air was choked with dust, sweat, and the blood of the combatants. The area in front of the line of soldiers became littered with dead and dying fighters. The horses and wyverns became an obstacle as the soldiers attempted to retain their positions in the line. The dead, the dying, and the bodies of animals forced them to clamber over just to hold the line.

It seemed like an eternity, but in reality, the battle was already won. The Ápastil were no match for the foot soldiers. They were a fine calvary, but they were used as swordsmen. Beyond the soldiers, they could see the countless dead horses, wyverns, and foes littering the ground. Stephan's men began to dispatch the wounded Ápastil by sword. As for Stephan, he ordered that his wounded men be tended for their injuries, while the horses stabled in the cove were brought forth. The remaining foes had already fled to regroup with the hordes in the north. "Hurry, now. We must make haste to the ferries," Stephan commanded. He was saddened that he had lost fifteen men with about 120 wounded. Then he came to realize that he himself was wounded as he felt warm, wet ooze running down his leg. Looking down, he saw a nasty deep gash wound to his left leg. He supervised the men as they assisted the wounded to mount their horses. He used a mage bandage on his wound and mounted his steed.

The column had finally arrived, and they were eager to see that two ferries were waiting. "Take the injured across first," said Stephan in a weak voice. "Grab the first priest or paladin that you see. Take the men to be treated for their injuries." With the two ferries, he was able to transport ninety at a time. Five ferries would be required to transport his men to safety. "Have . . . more ferries dispatched . . .

when you reach the docks," faltered Stephan as his breathing seemed shallow. A soldier suddenly cried out, "Sire, you're wounded!" seeing the blood dripping from his leg and the steed's saddle. He offered to assist Stephan to dismount, but the soldier was rebuffed, being told that his men came first.

Ultimately, the last ferry was being loaded with the remaining men. In the distance, they could feel the ground shaking from the stomping from the horde invaders. Stephan was slumped forward as his steed was led toward the ferry by its reins. The loss of so much blood from his wounds was taking its toll. As the last ferry debarked, Stephan wobbled and fell with a sickening thud onto the ferry deck. Several soldiers rushed to his side, but alas, there was nothing that could be done. "Tell"—he gulped for air—"tell Baldur . . . I have failed him . . ." and the breath of life had left him.

Agnar had relinquished possession of Mjolnir to Bogamaður, with a deep feeling of relief on his part. For over an hour, the dark elves held counsel over Helgi the Gray, Agnar, and Afmyndur. Messenger runners had already conveyed the news of the demise of Fort Windswept and that war was now upon the inhabitants of the southern realms. The Lava Pass gates had been reopened, and swarms of the despised Orcs and ogres were on the way toward Fort Hermana. The council was not eager to engage combat, but reality painted a different picture—the elven people had been thrust into war, whether they like it or not. Bogamaður addressed the council, "You have been true to your word, Agnar. We must not falter and dishonor the words of the elven people. Aye, we will fight side by side once again as an ally!"

Bogamaður was a good leader and showed his skills at decision making. He had a plan already ready to go, and he didn't hesitate to take advantage of it. Seven hundred elven archers were to reinforce the fort, and nine hundred was to sneak attack via the northern realms and come at them from the rear of the evil ones. Bogamaður and Agnar were within the second group, which was to attack swiftly at the horde's rear. Like any great leader, Bogamaður listened to Agnar's plan: feint an assault then peel away toward the Sko Forest, straight into the vines. *Use the carnivorous vines to our advantage!* Bogamaður liked the idea—create chaos within the Orcs' ranks *and* fight them, stir up the clouds of war. The races of men and elves were reunited once again for the common good. One army advanced to the north, the other, with Helgi the Gray and Afmydur in their ranks, toward Fort Hermana.

Dabbilus had to avoid the marching ranks bearing down from the Lava Gates. It delayed his journey to the Gate-Pass stronghold, but he arrived eventually. The sentries were surprised to see a single paladin approach the gates, but after stating his business with Rikard, he was allowed entrance. Commander Rikard greeted Dabbilus, and after exchanging the latest news from the war, Dabbilus brought up the reason why he was here. "Aye, great news. Saves me the trouble to scour the mountains. I can use the men if they join our cause. D'nno, but me thinks the invaders be heading straight to Castle Vokva," exclaimed Rikard.

"Aye, me thinks same. Lava Gates be open now, but rumor has it that some from the north broke off and headed for Fort Hermana," said Dabbilus. "Can ye spare some fur coats? Gifts for their leader, worked for me the last time I went to Jarnsmiða."

Rikard thought of it for a moment and said "Well . . . 'ava shortage of supplies here . . . I can spare a few leather goods, but no weapons or armor."

While waiting for the riches for the bandits, Dabbilus recounted his harrowing experiences in

Jarnsmiða. He choked on the words when he recalled how Smari had met his doom. Rikard tried to console Dabbilus and thought better of it. As a professional soldier, he too had sent men to their deaths as this was the way of the world.

Dabbilus exited the citadel and turned toward Jarnsmiða. *Better keep an eye out for Yeti,* thought Dabs. Soon, the Great Forge City was within eyeshot, the place where they had encountered the bandits. Staying mounted, he surveyed the area littered with boulders that had fallen from the mountain. Cupping his hands around his mouth, Dabbilus called upon the unseen audience with a "*hallo!*" Silence, except for the echoes that shot back from the mountain. "*Dabbilus here!*" tried Dabbilus again. All he got in return was the reverberations from his own voice. Dabbilus sat motionless upon his steed and pondered what to do next. Suddenly he caught a slight movement behind a boulder. "Dabbilus here. I have some supplies for you," said Dabbilus toward the boulder.

"Aye, I remember you. What'cha want? I thought you'd be dead by now," said the unseen person.

"You do know that Orcs and their allies have attacked the realm, and the commander at Gate-Pass has been replaced. Come down, we have much to talk about," retorted Dabbilus.

"Where'ya companions, the ones with you last time you were here?" came a question from the boulder.

"I came alone. This is no trick. If you want the supplies, you need to come to me. We need to talk," said Dabbilus.

Three armed bandits emerged, eyeing Dabbilus in a very suspicious manner.

Dabbilus was blindfolded and disarmed, and then the bandits led him toward their hideout, using the ravines and backtracking lest they were followed. Upon arrival, his blindfold was removed, and standing in front of him was a middle-aged man in disheveled, worn clothing. He had a brownish shoulder-length hair and an unkempt short beard. "Dabbilus be me name, a paladin by trade." Dabbilus bowed.

Without giving a name he asked, "What *exactly* do you want? Why are you here?"

"Aye, now 'tis the rub. You *do* know that the northern realm has attacked. It will be just a matter of time 'til they find you, and they will kill the whole lot of you. I have a proposition to make: Join me, return to Fort Gate-Pass, and I will have your records made whole again. No charges be forthcoming, no investigation into your criminal path to be mentioned again. Join me, and I will have your honor returned. No lies or deception by myself."

The leader of the bandits scoffed and asked, "And how do I know that you are a man of truth? Join you and rot in a dungeon somewhere. I'd rather take my chances here."

"Me lad, *I am a paladin*, an honest and honorable soldier serving King Magnus. I am offended by your remarks. You can stay, aye, ye can stay here, but I swear by the gods that there is no dungeon awaiting for you. Dost thou need me to swear to you an oath? Join me, and be free of your past. Join me, and live to return to your homes and families. Join me, and I will restore your honor. To that, I am willing to swear an oath to you."

The mages created two portals within the castle. One of the portals led to Cape Fear Landing, the other to Ferry Landing. Gormur was supervising the loading of the Skjaldbak with necessary supplies into the portals. Each portal was manned with three summoning mages to hold the portals open. Six Skjaldbak were completed and ready to go when the order was given. Three Skjaldbak for Cape Fear and three for Ferry Landing—more were being constructed as Gormur were busy at the task of supervision. Each Skjaldbak would be manned with three volunteer gnomes, a pilot, a boiler tender, and one with a blunderbuss.

The coal had been transported via portal, enough to run the Skjaldbak. Of course, the dwarfs continued to mine the precious ore; without it, the Skjaldbak was dead in the water. Spare parts had been constructed so that the gnomes were certain they had enough to fit their purposes. The time has come to just do it! There wasn't any time for test runs or tinkering with improvements. The time was to transport the boats, and with that, Gormur gave them the authority to begin the transports.

The Skjaldbak were appearing within the portals, and just as one arrived, the gnomes and the villagers had conveyed them into the water next to the docks. In the distance, the warships of the northern alliances had already set sail toward Ferry Landing with their majestic sails full of energized air. Using their looking glasses, they could see the sails long before they observed the boats.

The crews had already been instructed as to how to sink the chunky sailboats. As the clippers had to use tacking methods to move throughout the water, the Skjaldbak didn't have to because with the ingenious bifocal of individual propellers, the Skjaldbak could turn within a snap of a finger.

The Skjaldbak set to sea from the docks at Ferry Landing to intercept the schooners from the northern hordes. Skjaldbak from Cape Fear Landing set their sights toward the fjords between Bátslipa and the peninsula, which contained Fort Laekur.

Fort Laekur greeted the men from Fort Windswept with open arms. They were galloping toward the fort with banners flying. Baldur dashed to greet the newcomers, eager to hear of news about Fort Windswept. He broke his pace when he observed Stephan was draped over his steed, then he fell to his knees saying, "*No*, no, this cannot be . . ." with excitement and pain in his voice. The second-in-command under Stephan dismounted his horse and ordered some of his men to take the lifeless body to the center of the fort. The lieutenant offered his consolations toward Baldur and offered a helping hand.

"Sire, reporting for duty," to which Baldur did not respond back. "Sire, begging your pardon, but we still have some wounded soldiers at Bátslip. With your permission, I will lead a company back there. The militia there is no match for the Orcs."

Baldur seemed to ignore the lieutenant for a moment and then replied, "Very well, after the funeral, you can take leave. Place Stephan on the table over there and gather some wood. Let's send him off as a hero among men. We will meet again in

Valhalla, I swear it, and I will be a servant to you, a giant of men, Commander Stephan!"

The pyre was lit with Baldur saluting toward Stephan. It was a somber occasion with nobody talking. "This is the price of war. Good-bye, my friend," stated Baldur to no one in particular. After the service was performed, Baldur instructed to increase the patrols toward the peninsula water's edge. Baldur was hoping that the defenders would get enough time to counterattack should any hordes hit the beachs. The soldiers of the company were disappearing from view, headed toward Bátslip.

The news coming back from the warfront was solemn, to say the least. The message runner said that thousands of Orcs, ogres, and trolls had opened the Lava Gate and are streaming toward not just Castle Vokva, but toward Fort Hermana as well. The good news was that the elven clans had rejoined the war effort, but would they be on time to assist? That was the question; that was indeed the question.

Before them was the ancient Lava Gate, pitifully ajar, with columns of Orcs, ogres, and trolls trickling toward the south. Agnar and Bogamaður beheld a sight that they never dreamed possible: the gates of the gods thrown aside. Bogamaður yelled, "*Charge!*" With his bow drawn out and fitted with an arrow, he chased down a troll, and with a thump, the arrow found its mark. *Twhump*, *twhump* as two more arrows scored the target, and he watched the troll drop to his knees. Thousands of arrows lined the air as the elven archers made quick work of the seven trolls guarding the gates. The two dozen ogres watched in dismay as the troll and ogre sentries fell one after another. Ogres, in contrast to the Orcs, either fled or didn't know what to do as the Orcs were the commanders, not the ogres. They were good at following orders but were slow to grasp what to do. The gates were under the command of the elves within a few minutes. But the damage had already been done. In the distance, Bogamaður could see the trolls drawing catapults and rams while even farther ahead were the Orcs and the ogres. Agnar shouted, "I'll draw the stragglers toward the mountain foothills, just as planned. You pick off the trolls towing the catapults heading toward the castle! Take a hundred with me, you take the rest!"

For hours, Agnar and his men dogged the minions from the north. Then he saw, in the distance, the flaming meteors flying up to the heavens and fall upon the beleaguered fort. Agnar spotted the elephants, bearing toward them perhaps. He saw two dozen elephants with riders and closing fast toward them. Keeping just out of range of their assault, Agnar taunted them and drew them into the fen, which was laden with vines. Just as they broke off the attack, Agnar attacked again with a volley of arrows, enticing the foes to chase them, and then retreated, like a game of cat and mouse. As the pursuers approached the fen, Agnar and his men had disappeared into Sko Forrest. The elephant riders were inexperienced with the vines, causing panic and a loss of control over the elephants. Elephant after elephant was goring the next available target but to no avail. The constant barrage of arrows from Agnar and his men was too much. All of the elephant riders were destroyed as a fighting force.

Helgi and his men arrived upon a hilltop with the staff of his beaconing the way. The fort below was totally surrounded with volley after volley of fire rocks from the catapults. There were about thirty elephants attempting to dismantle the fortress walls using their tusks and trunks. One by one, the buildings within the fortress and in the village were being reduced to rubble. Now, only broken walls remained standing: Boar's Inn, the command post, the housing of the villagers, all of them were crumbling. With a sickening *thump* noise, a meteor landed inside of the tent city. Refugees were running everywhere with screams of fear as they scoured the fortress grounds for safety. Smoke and dust were choking the defenders. Everywhere, *zings could be heard* as arrows fell amid the beleaguered members. The air was filled with molten rocks from the catapults. The airborne splinters of wood from the fortress walls caused massive casualties. The shouts from within and without the fort were deafening—the cries for help from the wounded and the dying. Half of a section of the defending wall had fallen, now teeming with Orcs and ogres. Gagns was on the frontlines, directing the Konglos to seal up the breach.

"*Take it to them*—the Orcs first! Destroy their command and control!" shouted Helgi the Gray and spurred his steed forward. While elven archers showered the area around the breach in the wall, dropping scores of foes, they pressed on toward the beleaguered fort. Targeting the Orcs, the elven warriors pursued their quest of breaking the siege. With a mighty roar, thunder from a meteor soared ahead and landed with a sickening thud. Using his staff, Helgi smote down an orc who was trying to stab an elf in the back. Slowly but surely, the reinforcements had attained the liberation for the fort populaces. There were thousands lying on the ground, both attackers and defenders. Everywhere were the carcasses of horses, wyverns, elephants, and Konglos. The screams and moans of the wounded sang a tune of death, and the smells from the combat was sickening.

Attacking from the rear of the invaders, Agnar and his men had reached the frontlines of the combat. Agnar used Bangsi to assist as he fought hand-to-hand combat along with the elves. Bangsi tore off arms, legs, and heads from the vile ones, while Agnar devastated them with his bow. The elves were equally brutal as they fought their way into the fort. The elephant rider formations were shattered, eventually limping away from the fight. The catapults were set out of commission. Either they were destroyed, or the trolls which manned them were killed. The rain of boulders from the skies tapered off and eventually ceased. The siege had ended, but the suffering was nearly insurmountable. The black clouds of smoke from the buildings were choking as survivors attempted to put out the flames. The battle-scarred ground was starting to fill up with crows, buzzards, and vermin, getting ready to feast. The priests and paladins could be seen scurrying about, attempting to tend to the wounded.

Kaldhjarta was pacing back and forth, listening to Svaramin describe the efforts at the warfronts. The gnome realm was nonexistent now; the Orcs had effortlessly dismantled the country. Sanctuary Verslan had been sacked and the invading Orcs were busy plundering the city. It had not been confirmed, but he had rumors that King Smakongur was slain by one of the orc commanders. With a smug posture, Kaldhjarta seemed to enjoy what he was hearing. "With Fort Windswept out of the picture, now we can travel freely about. We can muster troops for the invasion of the south," said Kaldhjarta. "Continue with your report, Svaramin."

"Sire, the Lava Gates has reopened, and as we speak, there are tens of thousands of our troops streaming toward Castle Vokva, but . . ." Svaramin tapered off. "But I have unpleasant tidings from Fort Hermana."

Kaldhjarta snapped his head toward Svaramin and coldly said, "*Unpleasant tidings?* And what does that mean? Out with it. Exactly what does that mean?"

"It appears that the elven clans have rejoined up with the southern realms. We took heavy losses just outside of the Lava Gate, and entire elephant rider formations fled or have been killed. And that accursed Helgi the Gray appeared which bolstered the fort. The fort was spared," faltered Svaramin. He appeared ready to sob an apology as he was obviously afraid of the wrath of Kaldhjarta.

Contrary to his expectation, Kaldhjarta issued a statement which shocked Svaramin. "So! I was expecting Helgi to meddle. The burning question I have for you is: *What about Vokva*? I want those pious dwarves eliminated to the man! If Vokva falls, so do the southern race of men."

Svaramin was red-faced, and he bolstered himself up. "Sire, the invasion of Vokva is working as planned. Hearthglen will probably send reinforcements, but we can cut them off before they reach Vokva. I need to return to Svartaturn to supervise creating new troops. I expect that it will be done before columns from Hearthglen approach, well out of the reach of Castle Vokva."

Kaldhjarta added, "And what of the ships? We need to capture Cape Fear and Ferry Landings. If that works, we can use a tri-frontal assault on Vokva."

Svaramin bowed graciously. "The ships should take sail as I speak, sire."

Ferry Landing was teeming with activity. Hundreds of soldiers were swarming in the village, which comprised the docks and the dwellings. Before the portals had been activated, King Magnus created a new department, the naval department, and appointed its first admiral. Most dwarves scoffed at the idea. Whoever thought that the dwarves would need a navy, let alone an admiral? After all, the navy only had six boats in its fleet. He had appointed Jon Eriksson, a gnome in Castle Vokva, who had been employed to construct the Skjaldbak.

Scurrying to load up the Skjaldbak, the gnomes were scampering here and fro, getting the boats seaworthy. Admiral Jon could see the tips of the sails of the enemies using the looking glass. Gathering his sailors onto the docks, he said, "Seems like it is time for some action. High tide will be at 10:00 pm tonight, we will use the darkness to our advantage. Ram the ships midway of the vessel, reverse course, and target the next ship. Use your blunderbusses to shoot at the crow's nest. Do not stop, just ram and sail onto the next target. If they board you, use the blunderbuss to shoot them off the Skjaldbak. Try to sink them in deeper waters. We don't want any of them swimming ashore. If the enemy heads toward the Skjaldbak, we will steam out toward them. If they are coming toward Ferry Landing, attack. You've your orders." To that, the Skjaldbak were loaded, the steam boilers were ignited and ready to set sail.

The Skjaldbak were almost invisible as they were so low in the water. The only evidence that they were there was the steam coming from the exhaust pipes. The waves washed over the Skjaldbak like turtles, slow but steady. For over an hour, the Skjaldbak chugged along and Admiral Jon thought to himself that the first trials at sea are working! Now, for the second trial and Admiral Jon crossed his fingers as the first line of the twenty-five enemies' boats was coming up and fast.

With the darkness covering their approach, the first ship didn't even know what hit her. The crew of the Skjaldbak couldn't hear the screams and panic because the boiler and screws was deafening within the boat. The Skjaldbak lurched as the enemy ship was taking on water. Ogres and Orcs were thrown into the ice-cold waters, many drowning because of the weight of their armor. The Skjaldbak reversed its engines, ripping out much of the hull of the wooden ship. The next schooner was targeted, and the sailor manning the blunderbuss popped up from the hatch, looking for the crow's nest. The Skjaldbak eyed the enemy ship as a predator playing with a next meal. The sailor fired his shot with dismay as the crow's nest was out of the range of the weapon and ducked back inside of the Skjaldbak. Panic ensued within the crew of the foe's ship; they obviously had no clue as to what *or what* was attacking them. The rams of the Skjaldbak stung the vessel as the enemy ship was mortally wounded and began to tilt. Hundreds of enemy crew members were in the water, heading for Neptune's underwater realm.

Enemy firepower was useless against the Skjaldbak; the arrows and spears and even the onboard catapults were ineffective because the armor plating rebuffed everything that the foe threw at them. The ships from the northern flock were defenseless to counterattack. With three Skjaldbak, the southern alliance decimated twenty-five. Fifteen ships were sunk, and the remaining ten were forced to retreat. It was estimated that 2,500 troops from the northern realm had lost their lives. It was a resounding success, and Admiral Jon recalled the Skjaldbak to Ferry Landing. Not one alliance sailor was injured in the affray.

Lady Zonda listened eagerly when the messenger runner was updating the queen. She showed relief as he recounted about the victory at Fort Windswept, but she only wanted to know about Baldur—scant news of him—as her main concern was to hear news of her beau. Of course, she was under no pretense concerning the war effort—to hear that the Lava Gates had opened and of the tens of thousands invaders who were marching upon Castle Vokva at this moment. But she was desperate to hear of Baldur. That, and adding the dismay over Stephan's death, only increased the tension within her. She had already decided that she would lead two companies into the disputed land between Hearthglen and Castle Vokva; yes, she would take the remaining veteran soldiers from the citadel to assist Vokva. The queen would not like it, but once Lady Zonda had departed, then there would be nothing anyone could do about it.

Lady Zonda couldn't sleep, tossing and turning with a thousand things on her mind. *If only Baldur would send me a message, perhaps a sign of some kind to let me know that he is all right.* Of course, this was silly of her because he had so many responsibilities worrying about the realm. As she sat on her bed, she uttered a longing sigh. She wondered if Baldur felt the same about her as she feels now. Lady Zonda summoned her maid-in-waiting, and until the servant arrived, she was thinking of what she should write to her mother.

Dabbilus led his six hundred bandits toward Fort Gate-Pass. Of the eight hundred able-bodied bandits, only six hundred volunteered to rejoin the alliance. It was a slow trek between the gorges and mountain passes, but they eventually made it. The sentries at the main gate unbolted the gates and allowed them entry to the fort. The bandits were uneasy, throwing glances around as if they were waiting to be apprehended. Commander Rikard was in the courtyard and threw an arm around Dabbilus. After welcoming Dabbilus back, Commander Rikard addressed the dilapidated bandits, "I welcome you, gentlemen. You are sorely welcome. As Dabbilus has explained to you, there will be no questions, no reprisals, and your honor has been returned to you. The queen has agreed to everything which you have been promised. Find you some quarters, and we will reequip you with armor. Again, I welcome you with open arms."

In the command post Dabbilus was conferring with Commander Rikard on how to utilize the new recruits. Dabbilus offered to lead them into battle, striking from behind the opponents. But this time, the tactics of hit-and-run should be used: force the enemies to withdraw from the citadel at Vokva and have them chase hundreds of foes toward their troops and away from the siege of the castle. Commander Rikard agreed, saying, "It sounds good, but we are so few, and they are thousands. I hope that reinforcements from Fort Windswept can arrive on time. I know that the fort to the east suffered many casualties, and I don't even know if they can even show up here in time."

"Maybe we can buy some time by using these tactics," said Dabbilus. "I know that it is a long shot, but we cannot just cower here while King Magnus is under siege. These men have skills of deception and hiding after years as wanted men. We can use such skills in combatting the enemy: terrorize the foe to weaken their forces."

Toward the west, the sun was slipping into its nightly slumber. Dabbilus gathered his men in the courtyard and addressed them. "Lads, now is the time to gather for combat. Many of you will not be returning home again, but I beseech you to be a man. 'Tis better to die on your feet not as slaves but with a weapon in your hand with chivalry, honor, and as heroes. I die willingly as a paladin. If the price is my cherished freedom, so be it. What say you? Will you wade into combat at my side with a weapon in your hand defending liberty? What say you?"

The bandits hoisted their weapons and yelled "Aye!" The bandits were united in the cause. The men, mostly clothed in mail or leather armors, again yelled "*Aye!*" as one voice. Dabbilus turned around, and he saluted Commander Rikard. They were going into the throat of hell with dignity and honor, going to combat.

The fort gates were agape as Dabbilus, with six hundred fellow soldiers, disappeared slowly into the night. Commander Rikard spoke sadly, "The gods be with ye—be charitable toward Dabbilus and his men."

Baldur stepped out of the portal in Cape Fear Landing. With a grin on his face, he was greeted by Magnus. The Skjaldbak had worked wonders, totally destroying the invaders' ships. King Magnus then informed Baldur that the siege had begun here at Castle Vokva. Thousands of enemy forces had set up camp just outside of the range of their weapons as an attempt to starve the castle before launching the actual attack. The caverns below had begun to accept the women and the children from the castle, but there wasn't any panic on the part of the populace. "We can last maybe a month or longer, but we've initiated rationing of foods," explained Magnus.

"What news of Helgi or Agnar—or Gagns and Foringi?" asked Baldur.

"Aye, Fort Hermana was almost destroyed—many casualties. But she survived it, and it is rumored that Helgi the Gray is leading some reinforcements toward us. Other than that, I have no news," replied Magnus.

Entering the courtyard, Baldur and Magnus caught a glimpse of Biggy and his Konglos. He was entertaining several goblins from the Great Forge.

"I guess that any reinforcements can't come from Castle Hearthglen since we are surrounded. This is indeed a bleak picture," said Baldur with a stoic face. Both Baldur and Magnus remained silent for a while. They scrutinized the outer walls and their defenses. "But I, for one, have not given up. I'll fight until my last breath remains."

All throughout the night were small skirmishes along the outer walls. Small bands of the enemies would sneak close enough to loose a volley of arrows and retreat, just to keep the defenders awake. The sounds of the encampments of the enemies wafted in the air. Drums were beaten, trumpets were blared, and there was yelling and screaming—all the standard tactics to demoralize the encircled castle. Slowly but surely, those types of tactics do sometimes work, when the defenders reach a point of hopelessness.

The reinforcements from Castle Hearthglen had encountered the Orcs just about the halfway point between Castle Vokva and Hearthglen. It was a small contingent of three orcs and about two dozen ogres. It only took minutes to overtake and destroy the monsters. With trumpets blaring and lancers bearing down on them, the Orcs never had a chance. When the battle was finished, Lady Zonda ordered, "Tend to the injured," as she goaded her steed up a steep hill. She wanted to scan the countryside, looking for more foes. Taking her looking glass, she detected some cloudy tufts of dust, apparently leading *away* from Castle Vokva. Someone is engaged in combat to the east. She rejoined her militia and said, "Let's take a look at what all the commotion is about."

Lady Zonda and her army galloped into the direction of the haze, and after stopping upon another hilltop, she scanned the area. "*Orcs*—perhaps two hundred strong. They are fighting someone who isn't from Hearthglen nor Vokva. They aren't wearing plate armor. *Wait*, over there. Is it elves? And his army isn't using tactics I recognize." Once again, she rescanned the battleground and shouted, "Sound the horn! Battle formation! *Charge!"* At full gallop, the combat arena was a mass of Orcs, Ogres, and Elves, tangling in arm-to-arm fighting.

The men from Hearthglen crashed head on into the elves and the Orcs, with broadswords swiping the air around their greenish foes. Lancers, now dismounted, were running at full speed with their lances stinging the enemy forces. Grunts, screams, and howling filled the air. The ground was soaked in blood, and footing was slippery as soldiers from both sides were engaged in mortal combat. Like a swarm of wasps, the Elven archers loosed volley after volley of arrows upon the orcs and the ogres. Swordsmen from the three camps—men from Hearthglen, elves, and those from the northern invaders—were hampered by stumbling and falling because of the countless bodies from their compatriots. The sounds of clanging and thumps from their shields, armors, and metal swords impregnated the air. Lifeless bodies were everyplace: horses, swordsmen, elves, Orcs, and ogres. Soon, the combat was finished. The army from Hearthglen had lost thirty-five men, the elves about forty-seven, and all of the foes from the north.

Bogamaður searched out for the leader from Hearthglen. When he found him, he wanted to thank the army from the south. When the leader removed her helmet, he was shocked to find that the leader was a girl! He regained his composure, knelt on one knee, and offered his thanks. After introducing himself and his army, he said, "If you are going to Castle Vokva, you may be too late. The castle is under siege as we speak. Half of our elves had pursued the demons toward Fort Hermana, but I have no news if they are still living."

"Fort Hermana still lives. I know nothing as to their fate," replied Lady Zonda. "If only Helgi the Gray were here for good counsel," she added.

"Helgi the Gray was within our group, which was supposed to reinforce the fort," uttered Bogamaður.

"What to do now? If Castle Vokva is under siege, how do we break through the enemy lines?" asked Zonda.

"For the time being, let us rejoin as one army. I know there is a place just to the east of Vokva where we can tend to our wounded and rest up. Do you have any paladins or priests in your company, Lady Zonda?"

"Yes, we have both paladins and priests, and it gives us time to plan our next movements then," replied Lady Zonda.

The army of men and elves were camping within a secluded location where they were resting from the day's battles. Just after midnight, when the sentries had been posted, a man stealthily crept into the tent in which Lady Zonda was sleeping. He cupped his hand over her mouth and whispered "shush" with a finger over his lips. He said, "You have nothing to fear from me. We are from Fort Gate-Pass. There is a strong element from the northern allegiance which is nearby. Douse your campfires and have everyone follow me."

Having been so surprised about how this man could have eluded her sentries, she put a face on of questions. She nodded and silently crept through the camp, dousing the flames and gently shook the troops to wakefulness. Once the troops broke camp, they followed the silent man into the darkness.

After a two-hour walk, creeping into the gullies and ravines, the troops arrived in a camp where some six hundred odd men were lounging about. Dabbilus approached Lady Zonda, bowed, and introduced himself. He stated that he was trying to get to the castle Vokva and asked her business in this area. He added that the men with him were rogues and work for Commander Rikard. She grinned and said, "I know him personally and Baldur too! My mother, the queen, will be most appreciative if we can break the siege of the castle."

"Aye, me too. I long to rid those northern monsters from our soils. My rogue troops can take out twenty or twenty-five every time we sneak into their camps. They are almost invisible, and when they are detected, it is too late," said Dabbilus.

"We were trying to hook up with Agnar and Helgi the Gray from Fort Hermana to the east," interjected Bogamaður.

"Aye, I know both of them personally me-self. Should I send a couple of my rogues to make contact?" asked Dabbilus.

"Wonderful," exclaimed Lady Zonda.

Dabbilus snapped his finger and picked six of his troops to search for the stragglers. "We need to be on the move constantly—we don't need a patrol to spot us. Our rogues will be fine, they won't be spotted, but with a big party like we have here, they will be right down our throats."

Agnar, Helgi, and Gagns were the reinforcement force from Fort Hermana. Commander Foringi could not provide many troops should the fort be attacked again. There were three hundred elves who volunteered to go. Commander Foringi provided 225 soldiers. Gagns had his sixty Konglos, and he estimated that there would be eight hundred men in total. He said that one Konglo was the equivalent of two soldiers. Add in Bangsi, which he counted as five soldiers. That was a strange lot—a wizard, elves, and a gnome trailing after—was 225 soldiers and a column of Konglos.

This odd assortment, which comprised the relief forces, had just passed the Lava Gates and swung toward the beleaguered castle. Agnar alerted the company that there were six men on horseback riding toward them. Using the looking glass, Agnar said, "Men, not armor-plated. No helmets, no visible weaponry. Odd—but at least they aren't Orcs or Ogres." Helgi and Agnar rode out to meet the strangers. They conversed for a few moments then rode back with smiles on their faces. "We have wonderful news, men! Bogamaður and his men are up ahead. Dabbilus too, plus a contingent from Castle Hearthglen. We are to follow them," beamed Agnar.

After a gleeful reuniting, a council meeting was called by Helgi the Gray. Much was discussed such as the latest intelligence from the rogue spies, if it was even possible to break the enemy's line and flee into the castle. Bogamaður was in favor of just continuing to whittle down the enemy forces. Dabbilus put in that with the stealthy rogues, they could attack by surprise within the enemy's camps. Dabbilus also said that with their Konglos attacking and the invisible forces within the camps, it would create chaos and confusion. "If we take out the Orcs with our poisoned daggers, the ogres will cut and run," added Dabbilus. He reminded them that there were about 150 Konglos inside the castle. "Cut them loose upon the enemy." Agnar was in favor of Dabbilus's plan. With the elven archers shooting from afar, then the catapults would be useless. The key to the whole plan was to take out the Orcs and then get the Ogres. The trolls would be of no use against a speedy assault on their part.

It was decided to adopt Dabbilus's plan, but they were to wait until just after sunset. "Scout the weakest point in the enemy lines, kill as many as possible within the camps, and regroup before we assault the lines."

King Magnus, along with Baldur, was consoling the populace of the castle. There was a strange cold that had consumed the castle. Not a lack of temperatures, but rather like when you get chills down your back. Everyone could feel it. Perhaps it was their imaginations running amok. "Ah, there you are. Care to share your thoughts for the evening?" asked Magnus toward Biggy. Biggy was tending to his Konglos with the help of a few goblin guests.

"Aye, 'tis as though I am drowning. Nay, not drowning, but rather a *feeling* like I am choking. Me stomach is all in knots," said Biggy.

Baldur acquiesced and said, "'Tis the night air, nothing to be alarmed about. We are all on edge, just waiting for the onslaught from the siege."

"Walk with us, Biggy. We all need some friends about at times like this," the king said.

All of a sudden, a sentry posted on the wall next to the drawbridge bellowed, "*Something is happening! To arms, to arms!*" Everyone was running to see what was happening. The orc horns were booming from everyplace within the enemy camps. It appeared as though the Orcs were fighting, but who—or what?

There wasn't anyone there. Baldur and King Magnus climbed the outer walls with swords in hand. Baldur snatched a looking glass from a sentry, and he scanned the countryside around the enemy camps. Suddenly, Baldur yelled, "Konglos—about thirty of them—they are attacking the Orcs!"

Biggy grabbed the looking glass and broke out laughing, "'Tis my Konglos! Gagns brought my Konglos!"

Then came the ear-piercing sound of the Horn of Thor! Dabbilus! "Muster the men! Biggy cut your Konglos loose upon them! To arms, to arms!" ordered the king. Running toward his horse, the king shouted, "Lower the drawbridge. We are attacking, not just cowering like little children!"

Then a line of soldiers appeared from the rear ranks of the Orcs. Leading them was Helgi the Gray with his staff searing the night's darkness with life-giving light. There were some banners bearing the seals of Castle Hearthglen being held aloft as the riders crashed into the enemy lines. The night skies lit up as a torrent of flaming arrows hurtled onto the enemy. Baldur led a company across the gangplank of the drawbridge with screams of "Onward! Attack! Attack!" Biggy, on Konglo back, was ordering his Konglos forward! King Magnus led his men straight toward a den of Orcs, hacking, slashing, and killing many. Baldur was thrown off the back of his steed as a spear pierced the horse. Without a pause, he rolled to his feet with his sword in play. Bangsi was without fear as he slew without mercy. Every man that had a weapon from the castle had joined in the fray, emptying the populace into the battleground. Lady Zonda took an arrow to her left arm but continued to fight.

In the background, beyond the Blafjall Mountain, Eldfjall belched, and the lava and molten rock lit up the night skies. The tremors quickly became earthquakes as the combatants were thrown off their feet. Terror was everywhere with the chaos and confusion between the fighting and the volcano. Many hundreds of Ogres had fled the battlefield with the trolls running on the heels of the Ogres. The tide was starting to change the shape of the battle.

Whoosh, whoosh—the flapping of the dragon's wings blew combatants off their feet. The terrible claws snatched soldiers from the earth and dashed them back to the ground. Its gaping jaws were plucking soldiers from their stances and bit them in half. Kaldhjarta had joined into the fray. He was a horrendous sight to see, with his coal black plate armor and helmet, swinging his flail around. Soldiers were swatted as if they were pesky flies. Kaldhjarta targeted Bogamaður, tossing defenders aside as irritating annoyances. "You have been a nuisance. Now I take you to your maker!" shouted Kaldhjarta.

"And I will teach you a thing or two about elves!" retorted Bogamaður as he unsheathed Mjolnir! The two were circling each other, waiting for an opening to attack. Kaldhjarta unleashed his flail against Bogamaður's left arm. With a crack of bone, his left arm fell useless on his side. With an irksome laugh, the flail scored again alongside the head of the injured Bogamaður as the life drained from his body.

Bangsi then leapt into action toward Kaldhjarta, gripping his arm between his massive jaws. Agnar flew to defense of his Sekhmet, and as he did so, he suddenly found Mjolnir between his fingers. Mjolnir was humming and sparks were flying from the golden blade. Just as before, the Great Sword was alive with a life of its own, but this time, it filled Agnar with hatred. Kaldhjarta threw Bangsi to the ground, and with a sweep of his flail, a cruel whelping sound came from the Sekhmet. Kaldhjarta had a sense of fear; it was showing in his eyes. The flail swung and missed. A back swipe of the flail had found its mark! Agnar was knocked down to his knees when Kaldhjarta came in for the kill. Suddenly, a whimpering Bangsi crawled toward Kaldhjarta, and he clamped his jaws onto the protruding leg. Sensing a last chance for an opening, Agnar leapt up, and Mjolnir was buried to the hilt in Kaldhjarta's back. All of a sudden pain—real *pain*—was coursing throughout his body, like a thousand bolts of lightning. His head was swimming with thoughts of Smari, Bogamaður, Bangsi, and his mother before he blacked out.

Spring followed summer, and it was now fall, and the cool nights would signal a new season soon. Björg and Agnar were married, and they were anxious to move into Blesugrof before the winter snows. But

Agnar was a changed elf, as if part of his soul had been ripped away. His lifelong dream that he had, to own a farm and train ferreters, never came to be. He was bitter, not in the way that he treated people, but bitter that the accursed Mjolnir had destroyed him. He never mentioned the Great Sword or the Rendering Wars again. Most people attributed that to the horrors of war.

The biggest surprise was when Biggy was crowned by the gnomish peoples for his heroic deeds in the Rendering Wars. People often say that King Biggy had given his old farm, Blesugrof, because he owed so much to Agnar, and that crowning was because of Agnar. That was the furthest from the truth.

The wedding between Biggy and SiSi was declared—an event no gnome wanted to miss. There was exuberance among the gnomish people, with celebrations galore, music, and dancing in the streets, and free-flowing ales. Everyone associated with the ending of the Rendering Wars was in attendance except for one—Agnar.

Gagns was offered to be a prince because of Biggy, but he declined. Gagns remained in Castle Vokva, tending Konglos. He never came back to Boar's Inn.

As to the evil empire in the northern realms, they ceased to exist after the falling of Svartaturn and Svaramin. People often wondered about the fate of Svaramin and Lord Kaldhjarta, but it is only supposition. Kaldhjarta was swallowed by the ground under the evil creature, as if the dirt could cleanse the malevolence. To this day, no one knows of the location of the Great Sword.

Baldur and Lady Zonda eventually became husband and wife, and they work for the castle. Both of them had enough of war and yearned to live lives of normalcy again.

Commander Rikard chose to remain at Fort Gate-Pass. Dabbilus was knighted by King Magnus and elected to serve with Commander Rikard in the fort. Dabbilus built a new military service, called Rikard's Rogues, which specialized in stealth, espionage, and black operations.

The dwarven community, under the leadership of King Magnus, declared the ending of the Rendering Wars as a holiday. The festive event was crammed with speakers, political figures, and music and dancing.

The elven realms considered it a day of mourning as a thousand elves had lost their lives by sacrificing their lives for the race of men. The elves once again became an elusive race, vowing never to engage alliances again.

Agnar rebuffed several visits from Baldur, Dabbilus, and Biggy, claiming that he was too sick to accept visitors. Only on two occasions did he see Helgi the Gray again. The visitations were polite and cordial, but the subject of the Rendering Wars was never brought up.

Ten years later, after the birth of his two sons and his daughter, Agnar became ill and lay feverishly in the bed for a week. He was incoherent most of the time, but his last episode was clear and lucid. "Elska mamma mín, er ekki tíma að koma heim? Mér langur að koma heim til þin" said Agnar, switching between tongues. "Smari, my dear friend—great to see you again," whispered Agnar. "And Bogamaður, nice to see you again. We will share a mug together soon." He smiled. "And who do we have here? Bangsi, my beloved Sekhmet—stop it, don't lick me you rascal, you," cried Agnar with tears of joy streaming his face. "Mama, can I come home again please?" And with that, the eyes became cloudy as life slipped away from Agnar. A silent peacefulness had enveloped him.

Agnar's funeral pyre was ill attended. Björg, the children, Afmyndur, and Helgi the Gray were the only ones present. Attired in the same dress as when he attended the party at Boar's Inn, it was a stately event. His weapons were laid upon his chest: a hero's farewell for a great elf. Afmyndur kissed Agnar on the cheek and said, "Farewell, my son. May the gods be with ye." With a shove, the raft wandered into the sea and was set ablaze.

Helgi the Gray took Björg aside and stuffed an envelope in her hand. His bright blue eyes were full of compassion and sorrow. She tore the envelope and retrieved the contents, not wanting to know the contents. It was a letter from Agnar to Björg and the children. It read in part:

My dearest wife and children:

I wish to divulge the truth about the slaying of Kaldhjarta. Many legends and tales have been recounted. Some of which are partly the truth; most of them are made up by daydreamers. Mjolnir is the curse that I have been forced to bear ever since I laid my eyes upon it. It was that day that all innocence deserted me. People with chivalry and just causes, true in heart, and honorable intentions are often forced by circumstances of not their making; people who choose a path in life itself, who have no control over events which they are forced into. Perhaps it is the will of the gods; perhaps it is fate or a combination of both. I am not making excuses for myself, but all the suffering, pain, and death were because of me and my choice. Mjolnir needed a cohort for its evil intentions. I was the cohort.

When I struck the mortal blow that killed Kaldhjarta, I felt coldness, a ruthless hatred for everything living. I also received a glimpse of the future of the world. It was then that I realized that the world would always be a cold, harsh place to be. In the world as we know today, there will be no more Orcs. They will be destroyed by the race of men. Perhaps not within the near future, but be assured that this will be: the race of Orcs will disappear. There will be no more elves as they will be displaced by men. Dwarfs and gnomish people will face the same fate. But even if there were no more Orcs, Elves, Dwarfs, or Gnomes, there will be always wars; the race of men strive for it, yearn for it, and create it.

The message is clear: Hope is the great truth of the cosmos. Without hope, life is meaningless. Therefore, I urge you to stand strong; do the honorable things in life, and bring up your children and their children's children in a decent and moral way. Fear not for what is to come because if you have hope, then you can change the world.

When I was a young lad, I used to relish the tales from the past. My mother used to hold and coddle me when she was reading the tales; she was teaching me of hope. "Once upon a time . . ."

Agnar

The End

GLOSSARY

- Ápstil—Race of humanoids, dark brown in color, known for their riding steeds. Ruthless and cunning, they are Bedouin in nature.
- Arnar—Fort Gate-Pass commander.
- Attafot—Biggy's giant konglo.
- Aura—Monetary amount. 100 aura = ten-sheckles.
- Bangsi—Agnar's wolverine sekhmet.
- Blafjall Mountains—Just south of Fort Hermana.
- Bleusgrof—Farm owned by Biggy.
- Castle Hearthglen—Capital for the humans.
- Closu—Agnar's horse.
- Dabbilus—Dwarven paladin, called Dabs for short.
- Dragonhead Inn—Inn in the Fort Gate-Pass village.
- Dwarves—Stunted humanoid with extraordinary strength. Generally, they live underground and create magnificent things using a hammer and a chisel. They work ores and gems from the ground, use forges, and are excellent armor producers.
- Einauga—One-eyed cyclops in the Forge.
- Elves—Race of inhabitants, pale-skinned with pointed ears. They are attuned to nature itself.
- Ferjalönd—Ferry and ports on the north.
- Ferreter—Hunter by trade in the military.

- Flugapets—Flying mounts.
- Foringi—Second-in-command at Fort Hermana.
- Gemshard Heart—Precious gems that are used to bolster armor.
- Gnomes—Knee-high (to a human) race that use science to invent. They are good in accounting, as well as in banking.
- Goblins—Race of creature (similar to dwarves in size) that is excellent working with the sciences. They are dark-green-skinned, with pointed ears and no hair.
- Gormur—Lead architect for Jarnsmiða Forge.
- Gufaheita—Steam-generated hot pits around geothermal areas.
- Hearthglen—the ruling castle of the race of men.
- Heitapipur—Steam pipes used by dwarfs in their forges.
- Helgi the Gray—Snjofell after was slain.
- Hestur—Mounts (can be horses, donkeys, cattle, eagles, in the case of good characters; can be fiery steeds, mountain goats, water buffalo, bats, rocs, in the case of evil characters).
- Humans—Race of people that are generally tall and good at military skills and organizational skills.
- Jarnsmiða Forge—Dwarven iron forge factory.
- Jokla City—North alliance city inhabited by orcs and trolls and ogres.
- Joldugrof—Farm north of Egilsstað.
- Jon Eriksson—First admiral of the dwarven realm.
- Kaldhjarta—Ruler of Vithheld; a dark, evil protagonist.

➤ Kingdom Jotheim—Kingdom of the gnomes.
➤ Komdu—Order the sekhmet to appear.
➤ Konglo—Spiders; giant web-weaving creatures.
➤ Loftur Hamarsson—Iron-forge dwarf in the Forge.
➤ Mage Bandages—Used by healers and constructed by bolts of mage cloth.
➤ Magnus—King of Jarnsmiða.
➤ Mjolnir—The Great Sword forged by the dwarves.
➤ Ogres—Race of huge heavy-set bodies, muscular with two fangs protruding from their lower jaws. They are rather slow intellectually and hard to agonize.
➤ Orcs—Race that is aggressive and militarized. They have greenish-hued skin, generally with two fangs protruding from their lower jaws. Almost always with a crop of black hair braided on the head.
➤ Ormskepna—Evil advisor.
➤ Rikard—Dwarf prisoner.
➤ Salim-Dug—Árapstil commander.
➤ Scandium—The Great Ore given by Thor for forging the Great Sword, Mjolnir.
➤ Sekhmet—Pet (can be cats, dogs, wolverines, bat, apes).
➤ Shiva—Sphinx of Jarnsmiða.
➤ SiSi—Biggy's girlfriend.
➤ Skelbaka—Outpost for the north alliance.
➤ Skjaldbak—Iron boat that runs low in the water, like a turtle.
➤ Sko Forest—Forest area where elves live.

- ➤ Smakongur—King of the gnomish people and the Kingdom of Jotheim.
- ➤ Stephan—Prisoner befriended by Baldur.
- ➤ Svartaturn—The new black tower used by Svaramin.
- ➤ Ten-Sheckles—Monetary amount used.
- ➤ Two-Fishes Inn—Tavern in Castle Vokva.
- ➤ Trolls—Race of inhabitants similar to ogres, usually used for manual labor.
- ➤ Vithheld—The castle of Kaldhjarta.